WITHDRAWN

I AM A BIRD

I AM A BIRD

Hope Lim

illustrated by Hyewon Yum

CANDLEWICK PRESS

I am a bird.

Every morning, I fly like a bird on Daddy's bike.

CA-CAW!

CA-CAW!

I sing like a bird on the way to school.

People wave and smile,

and the birds sing back.

One morning, I see a woman
with a blue coat and a big bag.
She is walking very fast.

She does not wave.
She does not smile.

The next morning,
I see her again
with the same blue coat,
the same big bag.

I do not smile.
I do not wave.

I turn and look
and wonder . . .

What's inside the bag? Where is she going?

Why doesn't she smile and wave?

Day after day, my birdsong stops
when I spot the blue dot in the distance.

"Daddy, I don't like her."

"She's just a lady taking a walk."

But what if she's not?

I hide behind Daddy's back when we pass her.

One morning, we are late for school,
and we don't pass the woman.

Then, near the end of the park, I see her.

She's whispering a song to the birds!

I turn and look until she sees me.
I smile and wave.

CA-CAW!

For Sophia, my soaring bird
HL

For my mom
HY

Text copyright © 2021 by Hope Lim
Illustrations copyright © 2021 by Hyewon Yum

First edition 2021

Library of Congress Catalog Card Number pending
ISBN 978-1-5362-0891-7

20 21 22 23 24 25 LEO 10 9 8 7 6 5 4 3 2 1

Printed in Heshan, Guangdong, China

This book was typeset in Mrs. Eaves.
The illustrations were done in colored pencil and gouache.

Candlewick Press
99 Dover Street
Somerville, Massachusetts 02144

www.candlewick.com